A short story
by

David Washburn

Kill ~~the bugs~~ For Me

Cover Design by Joey Powell / Mad Axe Media

Interior Design by Joey Powell / Mad Axe Media

Proofreading & Editing by Kaylynn Wurzelbacher

This story is a work of fiction.

Any names are a coincidence and locations are fictional.

Published by Burn Ward Publishing

www.WASHBURNWRITES.com

Instagram & Threads: @WashburnWrites

Email: DavidWritesStories@gmail.com

Published in the United States of America.

1 2 3 4 5 6 7 8 9

Dedicated to Larry Long Legs

ONE

The August sun is unkind to the cars that crawl along the highway beneath the clear sky. Rush hour is even more unforgiving as the late afternoon heat cooks anyone in their vehicles who aren't fortunate to have air-conditioning. Travis—who only recently got his fixed—idles in traffic, paranoid that the air in the car will stop working again on a hot day like today. As if sweating all day in a warehouse while stacking and tossing boxes weren't bad enough, he's grateful to have cool air blowing on his face while chatter ensues from a podcast streaming in his car.

The drive home is frustrating at times, but has become a reliable constant in his week as he knows what to expect when he clocks out and hits the road. He knows that when he rushes out the door at five on the dot and gets to the highway around 5:08—depending on the red lights he sneaks through—that he can expect to have a solid twenty five minutes of slow-moving highway slogging. This used to irritate Travis. That was before he was married to the love of his life, Lily. And before they had their daughter, Zoe. When she was born, everything changed. Suddenly his mornings were less about how much sleep he got, but rather how much he didn't. All of this despite him still having to work full-time. These chaotic snapshots of driving drama after a long shift somehow became a calming retreat where he knew he could listen to whatever he wanted, and for a short time didn't have to answer to anyone. No one asking him to do this or that, no one requiring his attention. Just him and the peaceful isolation in rush hour traffic.

His iPhone begins to buzz in the cup holder as the chatter from some actor's podcast is quieted. He pulls his eyes away from the standstill sea of brake lights ahead of him to glance down at his lit up phone screen. Lily's name pops up as the phone vibrates in a cup holder.

Travis closes his eyes and turns down the podcast as a held breath escapes him. He picks up the phone expecting to be sent on a detour to pick up diapers or something. "Hey, Lil. What's up?"

Travis! she screams, enough to make him tense up and wince.

"Geez! What is it? Why are you shouting?"

Where are you at? she asks. Her voice rattles behind her artificial calm.

Puzzled, Travis stares ahead as the cars continue to inch forward. "I'm on the way home. Lily, what is wrong?"

I just need you to get home.

"Lil, you know how traffic is at this time. What's the matter? Is Zoe alright?" Travis asks, trying to calm down his wife and her panicked voice. Her fear has him on edge as he wonders what could be going on. Maybe something is happening outside the house.

She's fine ... Travis ...

"Yeah, Lilypad?" he replies, doing his best to be grounded and calm.

I ... I can't move, she says. Her voice lowers to a quivering whisper.

Travis can hear the tears as she talks through the crying. Her breathing gulps of air through her teeth as her nose makes that vacuum noise to keep anything wet from coming out. He adjusts himself to sit more upright in the driver seat. "What is going on? Talk to me." Her breathing resonates through the phone. Travis waits for her to speak, growing more anxious, and maybe becoming a little frustrated. "Dammit, Lily, you called me. Just tell me what's happening already!"

It's back ... Travis.

Travis lets his foot off the brake to roll forward another three feet before stopping again. His chin sinks into his chest. His gut is telling him what this call is. "What's it doing right now?" he asks, annoyed.

It's looking right at me.

"Okay, babe ... are you listening to me?"

Mmhmm.

"I'm on my way home. I should be there in maybe five ... ten minutes."

Just come straight home. I need you.

"I'll be there as soon as–" Travis is cut off when he hears Zoe on the phone in the distance calling for mommy.

Zoe. Baby! Go back in there. Mommy will be right there. Zoe begins to babble and whine. "*Go! Get out of here! Now!*

Travis hears his daughter begin to cry through the phone along with his wife's shouting. "Whoa whoa whoa, babe. You've gotta calm down. Chill! That's our little girl. What are you screaming at her–"

Please, she interrupts. *Hurry.*

The traffic is easing up little by little with every few feet between illuminated brake lights. "I already told you, I'm coming home. I'll be right there. You have to calm down though."

I know, I know, I'm sorry.

"You're gonna scare our daughter. You gotta pull yourself together."

You're right. I'm sorry ... I'm just scared.

"You're scared? How do you think Zoe probably feels with her mother screaming at her?"

Travis. I said I'm sorry. I'm not trying to be dramatic.

"Oh, really? You're not trying to be dramatic? Calling me because you're scared of a freakin' ..." He stops talking to cool his jets before he goes into a tirade and makes things worse. "I will be home shortly. Sit tight until I get there if you can't handle this on your own." Travis hangs up, annoyed as he tosses the phone into the empty passenger seat just as he is nearing the exit ramp. His short moment of solace is disrupted and the rest of his drive is spent anticipating what he is about to go home to.

L ily stands on the closed toilet seat, knees bent in a half-squatted position to keep herself from falling. Her calves burn from standing so awkwardly and trying not to keep balance.

"Honey. Go play with your toys. Mama's busy," Lily says with a parody of her own voice. Zoe stands in the bathroom doorway with her face red, eyes watery, and bottom lip puckered out.

Zoe raises her hands, grasping open and closed as she reaches for her mommy. Her little feet step out onto the cold tile.

"Honey ... not right now, Mommy's sorry," Lily says as her heart breaks. She stands paralyzed by what watches her, leaving her feeling trapped in the small space. "Get out!" Lily screams as she bursts into tears.

Zoe turns and runs out of the bathroom crying and undoubtedly scared. The front door slams as heavy footsteps race into the house.

"Hey, hey, hey, baby. What's the matter?" Travis picks up Zoe as she pitter-patters through the hallway and right into her daddy's legs. He scoops her up and holds her close. "Baby ... you're crying. What's wrong?"

Zoe throws her arms around his neck. "Mama."

Lily listens, but her eyes stay fixed to the floor, between the toilet and the exit, where the thing that cripples her waits, like a festering parasite that only wants to devour her. She takes in deep breaths that rattle her chest between each slow exhale. "Travis," she calls out, with her best impression of not being petrified.

Travis walks toward the bathroom at the end of the hallway with Zoe clutched to him as he rubs her back gently. "It's alright sweetie, it's okay."

He stands in the doorway to the sight of Lily on the toilet. "Careful honey, that toilet seat tends to move around. Don't fall or anything."

"I need you to kill it!" Lily says as calmly as she can muster.

Travis lowers down to a knee and pries Zoe off of him and puts her down on her feet. "Honey," he starts, looking into her scared puppy eyes, "Can you be a big girl, and go find your *favorite* stuffed animal for me? Please, honey."

Zoe rubs her eyes with the back of her hand as she nods slowly up and down.

"Go get it while Daddy helps Mommy for a minute."

As Zoe cracks a grin and runs past Travis into the hallway, Lily screams.

"Shh, shh, calm down, babe."

On the floor, a common house-centipede, or thousand-legger, explodes from its stagnant position on the floor and quickly climbs the side of the tub as Lily climbs from the seat to the top of the toilet tank. The lid rattles and clanks under the weight of her shuffling feet. "Kill it, kill it, kill it!" she squeals.

Travis watches Lily dance up onto the toilet and then his eyes see the bug skittering out of the tub and up the wall where it stops in the corner, where the ceiling meets the wall. "Kill ... the bug?" he asks with surprise in his voice. An undertone of playfulness accompanies his words.

"Yes!" she screams.

"Babe ... come on, those things are virtually harmless."

"I don't care. I don't want it here. Those things freak me out," she says with her bottom lip scraping hard against her top teeth.

"Okay, okay ... but, you do know that they feed on other bugs, right?"

Travis's question is met with a cold death stare from Lily. "I don't care if they cure cancer. Please, stop playing ... and get it out of here!"

"Alright," he says with a smirk. "You're the boss." Travis turns to leave.

"No! Where are you going!?" Lily asks.

"I have to get something to get it, don't I?" he answers from halfway down the hallway.

Lily eases her way back onto the toilet seat. Her eyes stay locked onto the bug as she begins to be bold. Begins to be daring, planting one foot onto the floor as she makes a run for it, scrambling to the door with a shriek. She runs right into Travis' chest as he tries to get out of her way.

"Why didn't you just do that before?" he asks, holding back a laugh.

"I didn't want it to get me."

"Get you!?" Travis can't help but to laugh in her face. The situation seems minor and maybe even absurd to him, but the fear ... very real to her. "Well I'm glad you find it hilarious. You can laugh about it on the couch tonight."

"Calm down. No need to fight about an itsy bitsy wittle buggy wuggy, okay honey?" Travis says with a broom in his grip and a goofy grin on his face.

"Ha ha, real funny," Lily says, still watching the centipede.

Travis stands beside the bathtub holding the head of the broom up like a warrior posing with a staff. "Stand back, ma'am," he switches to an attack position. "This beast shall not pass," he says in a comically deep tone, peeking back over his shoulder at his frightened—and annoyed—wife in hopes to get a laugh from her. He does not. She stares at him, scolding as he waits for her to crack. She isn't amused.

Her eyes peel open as wide as they can without tearing at the sides as her eyebrows raise. She sticks her face out, looking at the bug and then Travis. "Are you just gonna stand there or are you gonna kill it?"

Travis's mood deflates, blowing a breath from his nostrils as he becomes annoyed all over again. "Yeah. Sure."

The centipede sits, still and in the corner, part of its body on the wall, and part on the ceiling. Innocuous and unaware of the danger it is in, it doesn't move at all. Travis stares at it, unafraid—but intrigued by its body that looks like it would gush if smashed. He imagines it smeared across the ceiling before determining his move. With its seemingly-infinite amount of legs and long body waiting for its swift and crushing demise, Travis still finds it terrifying to look at. Not as terrifying as Lily finds it though.

Travis positions the head of the broom into the groove of the wall and ceiling and with no more hesitation he sweeps the bug from its refuge. It flings onto the wall where the shower head protrudes out as Lily screeches once more. "Babe, chill, would ya?" Her high-pitched voice makes his shoulder raise to his ears as he nearly drops the broom.

"Don't tell me to chill!" she demands.

The centipede falls onto the floor of the tub and rather than reacting to kill it—like Lily so desperately wants—he watches it skitter across the bright white surface with impressive speed. Every leg moving like a symphonic orchestra that plays the tune to its own escape. Travis watches the bug carry its thousand legs into the drain and disappear to live another day.

"Did you get it?" Lily asks with a changed demeanor and fear overtaking her voice once more. Travis leans the broom against the wall and leans over the tub. "Travis?"

He steps away from the tub and goes to Lily and pulls her into a loving embrace. "Don't be mad."

She pulls away from him. "Why? ... What did you do?"

Travis's cheeks tighten as he grimaces. "It's not dead," he whispers.

"Where is it?"

"It crawled down the shower drain."

"Why didn't you just squish it, Travis?"

"I was going to!"

"You just stood there staring at it. What the fuc—" Zoe comes into the bathroom with a stuffed raccoon as she offers it to Travis. "What the heck?" Lily corrects herself.

Travis takes the stuffed raccoon from his daughter. "Thank you baby," he goes down to one knee, eye to eye and kisses Zoe on the cheek as he hands it back to her. "Here, see if Mommy wants the waccoon."

Zoe takes the raccoon to her mommy and offers it to her and Lily's outrage fades into a simmer as she smiles wide with tight lips. Lily takes the raccoon and looks at Travis. "Please ... can you just call someone or something?"

Travis snickers. "Can we just focus on the positive here, please?"

Lily grabs Zoe's hand as she holds the stuffed animal. "What's that?" she asks, not looking at Travis.

"The big bad super scary bug is gone."

T ravis lies in bed, sitting upright as the phone screen illuminates his face. Lily sits at her vanity rubbing lotions and creams on her arms and face. "I think Zoe is out for the night," she says.

Scrolling mindlessly, Travis gets pulled into what he's reading. "Uh huh."

Lily stands up, her spaghetti-strap shirt hugs and compliments her freshly showered body. She climbs onto the bed from the foot of it. "Soooo, I think you know what that means," she crawls up Travis's legs in a very playful manner. He gently moves his phone away from his face as her legs straddle him. She leans in close. "It means mommy and daddy time."

Her lips grapple with his as his hands run along her hips. "Mmm, I like the sound of that," he says.

Pulling away, Lily sits straight up. "I also was thinking too ... I need to apologize."

Travis admires how her nipples subtly smile at him through the fabric just as she is peeling the shirt off. He can't help but to smile back. "Apologize for what?"

She leans down, her breasts brushing against him, only exciting him more. She kisses his neck, and then pulls away. "For overreacting ... about the bug earlier."

His hands slide up her waist. "No, I think you were right," he says with his hand finding his wife's breasts. "I was just looking at info on the thousand-leggers before you ... interrupted."

Lily kisses his neck. "Mmhmm, what did you learn?"

He can't help but to close his eyes and fall into the moment as her warm lips press against his neck. "Well, they don't actually have *that* many legs."

She kisses his neck more, bringing her lips up, closer to his face. "How many legs?" She adjusts her hips, tightening herself around him.

"Mmmm," he says, involuntarily, knowing where this is going. "The house centipede actually only has thirty legs."

Lily freezes for a moment while Travis waits for more of her lips. "You know what," she says as she climbs off of him. "Maybe we should do this another time."

"No ... wait, what just happened?" Travis asks, confused.

Lily slips under the comforter and lies on her side with her back to him. "I just wanted to spend time with you and you still want to talk about bugs."

"Hold on ... you brought it up though, and I was only looking up bug stuff so I could put *your* mind at ease." Travis sits up, stunned as he stares into her back, only wanting her back on top of him again. "Babe ... come on, seriously?" He lies beside her and spoons her, pulling her close. "You know those bugs can't even hurt you, right? Don't punish me for something *you* started."

Lily rolls over and faces him. "Okay ... under one condition."

Travis kisses her forehead with his hand rubbing her waist and hip. "Name it."

"No more bug talk."

Travis grimaces. "I don't know," he says, struggling to contain a playful grin.

Lily's eyes light up with shock as her mouth hangs open. "You're such an asshole, you know that?" She pushes him onto his back and climbs on top of him again.

"Yeah, but I'm *your* asshole." Travis pulls her down and they kiss passionately. Lily leans into it and her hips begin to move in a way they both like. "But, Lil," he says between her lips landing on his.

"Yeah?" she answers, more breathy in her words as he is no longer focused on pillow talk.

"Have you thought about going to a therapist?"

Lily stops and raises up. "For what?"

Suddenly Travis is struck with the awkward feeling of possibly killing the mood—again—and his genuine concern for her wellbeing. "You know ... the ... well you told me not to say it."

Lily tightens her legs around him and grabs a pillow to hit him with. "Shut up!" She whips it at his face again with a coy smile.

Travis holds his arms up in defense to protect from her raining blows. "Okay, stop, stop!" The two share in the laughter for a second. "But, seriously. I think you should set up something ASAP, babe. Especially since we have decent insurance now."

Lily feels awkward now, sitting atop her husband wanting desperately to get out of this conversation. *Maybe Travis is right.* A sigh escapes from her chest. "No ... You're probably right. How about I make some calls first thing in the morning?"

"I think that would be a great start, Lil'."

She leans back down, extra close to his face as she reaches a hand down and grabs her husband intimately, eliciting a soft gasp from Travis. "Okay, good then." Her lips tangle with his, sensual and eager as husband and wife do what adults do.

FOUR

Lily manages to make the appointment that she and Travis had talked about. To their surprise, she was able to see a new doctor the same week. The days leading up to the appointment had Lily anxious, though. A new doctor meant being vulnerable and hoping not to feel like she's being judged or dismissed because she's a woman. She has had many experiences with male doctors and physicians where she could mention something troubling her and the responses being summed up as her *just being a girl.*

It is important to Lily that she has a female therapist, and someone who hopefully is sympathetic to her fear, no matter how silly it may seem to anyone else.

"Lily, it's nice to meet you," a woman, not much older than herself says as she comes out to the waiting room. Her plain clothes and dark green cardigan give off an aura about the therapist. A Calm and confident aura.

"Hi," Lily says as she stands. "Nice to meet you."

"I'm Doctor Webber. Come with me." Lily follows the woman down a hallway listening to her shoes click about in the echoey hallway. "We're just up here, I apologize for the messy office. I see kids sometimes so, you know how that can be." Doctor Webber turns into an open door office with an arm out, welcoming Lily in. "Please, have a seat."

Lily sits on a long pleather couch and takes in the room as Doctor Webber pulls up a chair. The office is clean and organized, which leads her to wonder what the apology for the messy office from her new therapist was for.

"So, Lily ... what brings you in today?"

A deep breath is pulled in as Lily's hands begin to feel moist at the thought of diving into this issue. The same breath pushes out like it was meant to soften the blow of having to be vulnerable. Like she already knows how silly it sounds, anticipating judgment and professionally concealed smirks as she opens up this part of her soul. "I have this fear of ... bugs."

"What can you tell me about your fear of bugs, Lily?" Doctor Webber doesn't miss a beat. Doesn't break eye contact, or so much as even have a tone in her voice to suggest this is as strange as Lily feels like it is.

Lily sits up straighter, adjusting in her seat as she clears her throat. She goes into the events that happened earlier in the week with the centipede in the bathroom. How she panic-dialed Travis knowing he couldn't simply rush home to squish a bug. How embarrassed she felt squealing when he got home and swept it off the ceiling. How her heart sank into her stomach when he told her it scurried away into the shower drain and how she hasn't showered without imagining the bug crawling up from the drain and climbing up her leg since.

"Have you always been afraid of bugs?"

"Well, I used to just not like bugs. Not exactly scared, but the last few years I just get this crippling anxiety when I see one even near me."

"I see ... Did something happen that caused this?"

Lily adjusts in her seat, finding no cure to her discomfort by doing so. "Actually, I've thought about this a lot. Travis knows, but I try not to talk to him about the moment because I know it will just become a thing we laugh about. And by *we*, I mean he."

"Well, tell me about it."

"Okay ... back when we first got married—before we had Zoe—we were moving into our first apartment. My mom and I were cleaning it before Travis and his cousin arrived with some of the furniture and boxes. It wasn't a great apartment. One of the perks to it was that if we cleaned it up we could move in and get a break on the deposit so we jumped on that. So I'm in the kitchen scrubbing the counter and when I finish I grab more cleaning wipes and I start to clean out the cabinets. I clean out two and they're dirty, crumbs and a smell that I can only describe as somehow dry and wet at the same time. It was the third one that it happened. I opened the door, really focused on the task, you know, in cleaning mode ... and I fell back screeching as a million roaches spilled out and got all over me."

"That sounds like the kind of thing that could traumatize someone."

"I scooted across the kitchen floor brushing them off. I could feel them crawling up my neck. Along my arms. I could see them on my leggings, flinging off as I swatted them away. My mom rushed over and didn't know what happened. All I know is that she looked over at the open cabinet door and covered her mouth at the same time I looked up and saw it. Roaches crawling and scattering inside the cupboard and falling onto the sink below, covering the countertop that I just cleaned. It was awful." Lily shivers. "I get the heebie jeebies just thinking about it now."

"How often do you think of that moment?"

"Anytime I see a bug," Lily snickers, shaking her head in disbelief of her saying all of this aloud. "I get cold chills anytime I open a cabinet door now—if I'm being honest."

"I see."

"There's more to the story ..."

"Oh, okay."

"So later that night we're in the bedroom. Travis just put the bed frame together and I had made the bed with brand new sheets. I grab one of the boxes and set it on the bed. This particular box was old sentimentals and things that my mom told me to take with me. It was sitting in my parents' garage forever. So I open the box and, all within maybe three hours, something even worse happens."

"What was in the box?"

"Spider webs. Lots of them."

"No spiders?"

"Have you ever seen those little white fuzzy balls that sometimes are in spider webs?"

"Oh no," Doctor Webber says as a frown takes over her face and her head sinks. She already knows where this is going.

"Yeah ... so I didn't know what those were then. So I grabbed one. I pinch it between my index and my thumb and it crushes easily but all of the spiderlings in the world come bursting out of that little spider sack."

"Well, no wonder you're so terrified of bugs, that would probably frighten most people. It sounds like you weren't having a great day at all in your new place."

"Not at all ... so I scream my head off and Travis rushes in, sees me stomping and kicking, arms flailing like some kind of lunatic."

"Well, that is awful, and you've been scared to do normal things ever since, huh?"

"Yeah. I guess so."

"Well," Doctor Webber starts as she uncrosses her leg and crosses the other. "I think I have a solution that I have seen success with in patients before, if you're open to trying with me."

"I want you to lie down. Get comfortable, you're welcome to take off your shoes," Doctor Webber says. Lily thinks about it, but chooses to keep her shoes on. "Lie still on your back and make sure you can breathe deep ... Now I want you to close your eyes."

Lily closes her eyes, becoming more anxious than relaxed as she waits for more information on what this solution is that Doctor Webber is so calm and slow about getting to. The thoughts race through her brain in anticipation.

"Have you heard of immersion therapy?"

"I have." Lily suddenly gets really uncomfortable thinking that she is about to be dropped into a bathtub filled to the brim with all sorts of crawling and slimy bugs.

"Okay, so this isn't quite immersion therapy," the relief Lily feels when hearing that is immediate, "but, we're going to use a visualization technique that is sometimes associated with immersion therapy. This is a really powerful tool in some cases when it comes to learning about our own psyches."

Before the thought is even suggested, Lily is in her head, standing on the toilet screaming at her daughter to stay out of the bathroom. The bug is much larger the way she remembers it and fights the urge to squirm on the couch at the thought of the bug looking right at her from the groove where the ceiling meets the wall.

"Sometimes overcoming your fear of something means you just have to push through it. Understand it. Sit with it, even if it's uncomfortable. Have you ever heard the expression, *the only way out is through,* before?"

"Yes."

"Well ... in this case you have to use your mind like any other muscle in your body, and train it to become what you fear."

Lily is already in her head, in the bathroom as Travis comes in.

"Now, Lily ... What I want you to do is," Doctor Webber's voice feels rich. Soft like the warm whipped cream on a hot drink from the local coffee shop. The deep sense of relaxation grabs Lily as her therapist's voice pulls her further into the moment. The voice is isolated and distant the way she hears her, but it's somehow invasive and intimate at the same time. "Walk me through the moments leading up to the last moment you freaked out."

Lily begins to describe what she is seeing and the moment in her mind takes over entirely. She relives the moment and all of the feelings and sensations are even more intense and present than before. Something about her being consumed by this retelling makes her head feel like she is underwater. The sounds around her are cloudy and muffled and even her own voice sounds deeper than her normal voice.

She takes in a gulp of air and as she releases it. Her eyes open and the muffled sounds in her head are sucked out from her ears and she is sitting in her car in the parking lot outside of the hospital. The disorienting feeling has her confused as she tries to catch her breath but feels as if she can't. The world outside continues despite her panic. The worry creeps into her head, now less about the bugs, but more about the time lost between her lying on the couch and being shaken up in the driver seat.

The next day.

Z oe is in the living room hypnotized as she sits on the floor with a bowl of sliced bananas and a sippy cup
watching Octonauts. During times like this Lily takes advantage to get some things done around the house. Laundry seems never ending, but she finds herself putting away the last load of laundry in her bedroom. She is getting preemptively excited as the last of the clothes are being stuffed into the dresser and hung on hangers for the closet. The idea of taking Zoe out for a walk seems appealing with her checking off the big item on her to-do list for the day.

With the empty basket on the bed, clothes folded neatly beside it, Lily slides one of Travis' nicer button-up shirts onto the hanger. The closet door hangs open, waiting for her to hang one last item. As she turns away from the bed and starts to take a step toward the closet, that's when she sees it.

Another one.

The centipede skitters across the carpet as a squeal escapes her. The kind of sound that might scare Zoe if she were in the room with her. The kind of high pitch vocalization that Travis might make fun of her for. She hops onto the bed, messing up the neatly folded clothes that were meant to be put into the dresser. She watches the pest run to the wall and then follow along the baseboard. Its legs—tiny to her—but large in scale to its own body move so fast. They move so fast and it looks like there are more legs than there really are as they work together in their complex mechanics. Lily always heard them called thousand-leggers, even as a little girl. Bugs had always grossed her out, but as she trembles in place, standing on their queen-sized bed all she can think about is Travis telling her that they actually only have thirty legs.

The centipede skitters along and finds its way into the dark closet. Lily's heart pounds in her chest so hard she can feel it in her ears as her heart rate picks up. The children's TV show plays cheerful upbeat music in the other room as the horror in the bedroom persists. She has to get to the closet but knows the bug ran inside. The bathroom thing was a little traumatizing, but it wasn't the worst time she reacted badly to a bug either. At least in the bathroom she was paralyzed with eyes on it. This time, she's paralyzed without knowing which part of the closet it's in.

The thought to call Travis enters her mind but she remembers how he made light of the situation last time and how it caused a riff between them for an evening. Lily would not be calling her husband anymore to come kill the bug. She knew that her best course of action was to calm herself down and to be strong for Zoe. This is a perfect opportunity to focus on what her therapist said about overcoming her fears. Sometimes the only way out is through.

Later in the afternoon Lily and Zoe are home from the park. After fun in the sun for about an hour, they're both plopped down on the couch while Zoe is already passed out sleeping, lying on her mother. Lily scrolls on her phone and finds herself getting ads for pest control and videos on social media with different types of bugs. The sight of them makes her squirm and she immediately scrolls right past. The ads must have been from her phone hearing her and Travis talk about it recently.

While Zoe sleeps, Lily fights off her own exhaustion by deep-diving on her phone. Something that Travis said to her the other night about the bugs got her thinking that maybe if she were to learn more about them, and understand them, that she may be able to overcome her irrational fear of bugs—even the creepy-crawly centipedes. This aligns with what Doctor Webber said as well.

It all starts with a simple Google search.

Do centipedes bite?

The search results come up quickly. Suggestions of what to search as she types let her know that this would be a commonly asked question. They do not bite, but they have hollow front legs used to pierce skin if they feel threatened. It isn't common though and they are more likely to flee than to outright attack. Reading about how painful that piercing could be doesn't do much to ease Lily's mind, but reading that it's rare for them to attack somehow does.

Her reading sends her down a deep and dark rabbit hole. Among photos of centipedes being portrayed as cute, others somehow seemed more menacing, even if they were just ordinary photos. Pictures of their scientific anatomy were only more terrifying, but with a more informed kind of fear. She learns about how they're drawn toward moisture and how sometimes a centipede might mean more and that it's likely a sign of a bigger problem besides pests. Even though they don't bite or attack, knowing this information presents a whole new concern and the anxiety stays high until she is able to talk to her husband.

SEVEN

Once a month—usually on a Friday—Travis meets up with some of his buddies from work after their shift for chicken wings and beer. He gets the okay from Lily, although every month when the post-work wings are calling his name he feels guilty knowing he is out with friends while she is home with Zoe all day, every day. That guilt is forgotten as fast as the beer is guzzled though. Once he arrives and the fellas are having laughs he's relaxed without a worry in the world.

With a couple of pints in him, and a pile of bones in a cardboard basket, Travis and his buddies aren't ready to go home just yet.

"So then, I come home from work. My wife is messing with her garden, so guess who has to take Kenny to baseball practice?" Travis' co-worker asks, mid-way through a rant. "This guy." He points both of his thumbs to his chest. "So I do all of that and come home, it's almost nine o'clock. I just worked all day and took my kid to his sports stuff, we're on our way home, and she calls asking me to pick up dinner … Can you believe this woman?"

Travis and the other two guys at the table shake their heads, unsure how to respond to their friend's complaints about his wife.

"You think that's something," one of the other guys pipes up. "I've been working overtime, man, almost sixty hour weeks. I'm tired as a dog. I'm making good money, right?" Everyone at the table feeds his fire with a chorus of *rights*. "You'd think with me working all these hours and making all this money, that I'd have somethin' to show for it … but guess whose spending all of my hard-earned money though?"

Travis takes a sip of his beer, holding it by the neck, nearly emptying it in one swish as the men chat (complain) about their significant others.

One of the guys at the table watches Travis as he sits as just a spectator. "Trav … you're bein' quiet over there. I know you got that baby at home and ya old lady. I *know* you go through it, huh?"

Travis sits the empty bottle on the table and answers in silence with his eyebrows raised. Travis always hated the term 'old lady' when referring to his spouse. It violated his sense of youth, and also undermined how he felt about her. She was still young and gorgeous and neither of them had surrendered to the idea of retirement plans or upgrading appliances as a highlight of their weekend.

One of the other guys notices the facial expression and joins in. "Yeeeah, my boy. I know your wife is probably always on you, ain't she?"

Travis snickers as he leans back. "Nah, she ain't that bad guys. I'm pretty lucky, all things considered."

One of his friends takes a drink. "Bullshit!" he says as he sets the bottle down on the table, keeping his hand on the bottle. "I know things can't be all picture perfect. What gets under your skin?"

Travis laughs, uncomfortably. "Nothing. She's great. Things are great."

One of the other guys leans in close with his elbows on the table, "Come on," he says in a whisper. "Every guy has *somethin'* they can't stand about their ole lady."

"Come on, man ... you ain't gonna tell us? Ya makin' us look like real assholes right now."

Travis shuffles in his seat, clearly wanting out of this conversation. "Okay ... maybe there's one thing."

"I fuckin' knew it!" one of the guys shouts, going for a high five with the guy sitting across from him.

"It's not all that serious, calm down," Travis says.

"Well don't keep us waitin', what is it?"

All eyes are on Travis as he has to tell them something to get them to let up. "She's scared of bugs."

The other guys stare around the table at one another. "So, don't all women hate bugs?" one of them asks. Travis immediately regretted it as he let the words slip, but maybe this would be nice to talk about with someone else.

"No ... Well, yeah ... I don't really know, but Lily is different. She *hate,* hates them. She literally called me the other day to hurry home so I could come kill a bug in the bathroom."

Laughter fills the air. "So she's just extra scared is what you're sayin'?"

Travis scrunches his face into an awkward smile. "No, it's way more dramatic than that. She won't risk it *getting* her and so she just freezes and freaks out."

"Why doesn't she just kill it?"

Travis shakes his head, realizing the absurdity of this gripe. "I don't know, I just know she won't and it has caused stupid fights more than once. Even when I try to make light of the situation it always makes things worse."

One of the guys shakes his head as he leans back. "Psssh, I get it bro. My lady is scared of bugs too, but damn! Your lady is probably scared to leave the house or somethin'."

Travis feels the pressure to keep it short and not say anymore but the unspoken need to explain further takes hold as he opens another beer and takes another swig. "I just don't get it. You know, when we first started dating, one of the first dates we went on was my buddy's boat and we went fishing. She didn't have any problem baiting the hook and touchin' worms."

"I don't know bro, worms don't bite or have legs though."

"Yeah, maybe it's just the bug with wings or the creepy crawly kind," Travis says.

A waitress walks up to the table. "You boys ready to check out? Can I get you anything else?"

Travis reaches for his wallet, eager to pay and get out of the nagging conversation. Feeling bad about complaining about his wife, he just wants to go home to her and his daughter that much more.

EIGHT

Lily's reflection is stunning as it stares back at her in the stylish dinner dress that she will likely only wear for special occasions with Travis. A night out sounds intoxicating as she longs to be wined and dined while someone else watches Zoe for the night. Parenting is exhausting and though she's beautiful in her provocative dress, she is still disgusted at herself. She used to be fit and thin and since having the baby every new curve or pound that climbs the scale in the bathroom taunts her. She pulls the dress off, offended at the betrayal of her body.

Standing in front of the mirror in her bra and panties, she studies herself. A private moment where her insecurities can roam free, even if they prefer to tear at her pride. A series of discarded dresses sit in a pile on the bed from her trying on one after the next, none of them offering her the confidence she desires. She goes to the closet, but despite her being in and out a handful of times already, she has the sudden recollection of the centipede running in there earlier in the week. Traumatized, she can't help but to shake off the shivers and move her feet. It doesn't help much that she never saw where it ran to and still thinks it's hiding somewhere. The idea of a tiny hole in the shadows is planted in Lily's mind. She imagines the centipede crawling into it to lay a bunch of eggs where those babies would grow up to run out and scare her even more.

She stands in front of her clothes, pulling a shirt from a hanger to pull it over her. Her anxiety can't stop magnifying the worst possible ideas. She looks down at her bare feet as cold chills creep along her arms and thighs, imagining things that very well could happen, even if unlikely. She uses her right foot to scratch the top of her left, picturing what those tiny little legs might feel like racing across the tops of her feet. The tickling feeling, like a thousand blades of grass in the wind against her skin. Lily shivers at the thought and can practically feel it as if it were really happening. Her feet shuffle and she runs to the bed and jumps, feeling like the safest place to be is to not have her feet on the floor.

Lily looks at the dresses that she cast aside and she laughs. Even in private, she hides her face in her hands embarrassed.

"Lily, get it together you crazy bitch," she says aloud with a smirk. The absurdity is never lost on her.

Just as she is drowning in her silly feeling, she hears Zoe. "Mommy!"

The anxiety dissolves and Lily takes a deep breath as she heads into Zoe's bedroom. Zoe sits on the floor with a variety of toys and a proper mess of things from a day of play. "Hey baby, whatcha doin'?" Lily asks in a comforting tone.

Zoe turns with a finger in her mouth along with something else that she's chewing on with a look of disgust that disfigures her expression.

"Whatcha eatin'?" Lily asks, with a more concerned look on her face.

Zoe turns away and starts to crawl across the floor as Lily jumps into *mom mode*. "Come here," she says as she reaches a finger into her mouth. "Spit it out, baby. Give it to Mommy." Zoe laughs, resisting the finger in her mouth, but Lily has her index hooked inside her cheek as she feels around.

That's when she feels the stinging hot pain on the tip of her finger. "Ow! Shit!" Lily curses, jerking her hand from Zoe's mouth. "I mean ... shoot!"

She looks closely at the tip of her finger where it's pulsating, only to see redness, but nothing else. Just the brief moment of pain. She looks down at Zoe to see her plop back down on her butt with a disgusted look on her face as she smacks her lips with her nose scrunched up. Pieces of a thousand-legger fall out of her mouth and onto her shirt before then hitting the carpet. The legs are still attached to pieces of the bug's body and still move like something small and animatronic.

"Oh, no, Zoe," Lily shrieks, crouching down to pick up her baby. "Let's get you something to drink."

"Yucky," Zoe scowls as her disgusted face quickly transforms into tears.

Tears quickly turn to agonizing screams.

Lily tries to comfort Zoe but the screaming becomes overwhelming in a hurry.

Travis sits in the parking lot of the restaurant for forty-five minutes to allow himself to sober up a little to avoid any danger behind the wheel. Granted, he didn't feel wasted, but he couldn't take any chances—after all, he has a wife and kid at home.

After a quiet and uneventful drive home, he walks through the front door to be greeted with Lily pacing around the living room. She holds Zoe like a newborn against her chest while bouncing her up and down and patting her back. The cries sound like something painful and Travis' instincts are to protect his child.

"Oh, good. You're home," Lily says with a wave of relief in her voice.

"What's going on?" Travis asks.

"She's been screaming for the last twenty minutes. I don't know what else to do," Lily says, defeated.

"Hand her here," Travis says, reaching for Zoe.

Lily hands her over. "She just started crying and I was trying to–"

Travis sits down on the couch as he holds Zoe close to him. "Hi Zoe Bear, why are you so upset? What's wrong?" Zoe calms for a moment and stares at him with her beet red face. "Baby, you're so hot," Travis says with surprise as he looks at Lily. "Have you felt her!?"

"Yeah, I have. Should we take her to the hospital?"

Travis sits Zoe on his knee and looks at her face and notices her mouth and chin swelling. "Let me have a look, baby," he says as he opens her mouth to see her tongue swollen too. "Shit."

"What?" Lily asks.

"I think she's having an allergic reaction to something. Did she eat anything unusual?"

Lily's hand shoots to her face as she begins pacing frantically. "She had … juice, crackers … apple slices. And–" Lily freezes, realizing how silly this is going to sound to her husband. The look on her face makes that apparent.

"What is it?" Travis asks with anxiety mounting.

"She actually ate … a bug."

"A bug?"

"Yeah … one of those thousand leg things."

Travis rolls his eyes. "Are you serious, Lil? How the hell did that happen?"

"I don't know. I came into the room and she was just sitting there chewing on it with a nasty look on her face."

"Did this just happen?"

"Not too long ago, yes."

"I think she might be having a reaction. We should take her to the hospital."

"I had to pick pieces of it out of her mouth. I got stung in the process too."

"This is just great," Travis says as he sits Zoe on the couch and starts grabbing the diaper bag. "Well, you aren't having any allergic reactions to it, are you?"

Lily is already grabbing items to take with her. "Not that I can tell. I'm more worried about her right now."

"Well the doctor will give her an antibiotic hopefully and we can just keep an eye on her. She has a fever too."

"Do you think that thing stung her when she was chewing on it?"

"I mean, if I was a bug, I would ... no different than stepping on a bee, I'd think."

Zoe has since stopped screaming but is still whimpering on the couch. Travis and Lily are quick to pack a bag and run out the front door to take her to the Emergency Room.

The front door opens as Travis enters the dark apartment and hits the switch. The living room fills with light as Lily follows closely behind with Zoe cradled in her arms, zonked out. Travis tosses the keys into a ceramic dish on a small entry way table near the door and lets out a big yawn as he slides his feet out of his shoes.

Lily sits on the couch as Travis heads into the bathroom. It's late and both parents are tired from the impromptu trip to the ER. Not much is said before Lily is dressing down Zoe and preparing to take her to her bed. Lily is wanting to go to sleep herself, especially after a day as eventful as the one the entire family has had. Zoe isn't too bothered by being undressed and put in her bed as she is on fever medicine and antibiotics that should have her resting through the night. Lily changes her diaper and Zoe opens her eyes for just a moment but goes right back to sleep with no hesitation. Lily tucks her in, gives her a kiss on the forehead, and leaves the bedroom.

Lily goes into the bedroom and sees Travis already laying in bed in gym shorts, on his stomach, snoring. She goes into the bathroom, thankful for the quiet moment of peace she always wishes she could have as she cleans herself up and hits the pillow hard not long after. The darkness in the room is like a cool welcoming hug and the silence an even more soothing song as she crashes hard.

Travis's voice tears through the house causing Lily to jolt up in confusion and panic. The screaming hardly sounds like her husband though, as his pitch is higher than she can ever recall hearing before. She gets on her feet with her heart already beating, trying to escape from her chest. "Travis!?"

Travis doesn't answer. He only continues to scream. "Get away! ... No! Stop!"

"Travis!?" Lily cries out once more, staggering out of the bedroom and into the hallway. Her feet twist beneath her sleepy body begging for balance.

"Just go!"

Lily follows the screams through the dark house. "Travis!? ... Zoe!?"

More screaming ensues as Lily passes the main bathroom, and then the third bedroom that they use as a makeshift office. Zoe's bedroom door is open and as she stands in the doorway Lily is not sure what she's seeing for a moment. Travis stands on Zoe's dresser with his palms and back against the wall while Zoe sits on the floor staring up at him. Her arms outstretched reaching for him to pick her up. "Stop it!" he screams.

"What is going on here?" Lily asks, genuinely unsure what she's seeing. Zoe reaches for her dad as he wears a petrified expression. Lily stumbles into the room, the carpet brushing against the bottom of her feet as she bends down to pick Zoe up.

"Lily, no! What are you doing!?" Travis interrogates.

"I'm taking her out of here before you scare her. You're scaring me with all of that screaming. What are you even doing?" Lily demands.

In a catatonic state, half awake with a heavy head and body, Lily goes to hold Zoe close to her chest like she always does. The same way any mother would comfort their child. Travis locks eyes with Lily, absolute horror stares back at her. "Lily ... what are you doing?"

"What are *you* doing?" she asks, annoyed, as she turns to leave the room. Lily holds her daughter close with a gentle hand caressing her back when she feels it. Like getting snagged on an exposed nail or something. She feels it against her shoulder and chest. "Zoe, honey, why are you pinching Mommy?"

Travis' eyes cut through Lily. Absolute horror painted on his face. "Lily. Put her down ... that's not our baby," he whispers.

Lily stares at her husband, steadying himself on the dresser with a face that can only suggest that he is being ridiculous. "You don't think you're over-reacting just a–" Lily turns to look at her sweet baby girl in her arms. The pinching continues and she pulls her away and at the very sight of Zoe, she drops her. Confused—and even more horri-fied—Lily stumbles back and falls into the wall, slid-ing down it as she covers her mouth to trap the scream that is desperate to escape.

Zoe lies on the floor, no longer screaming or cry-ing. Instead her voice whines softly, devolving into a sound that can only be described as a gurgling throat with multiple voices in unison. She writhes and squirms, her legs moving in a uniform motion. Lily watches with ragged breaths as her daughter rolls onto her stomach and raises herself up, not with her hands, but long, thin, protruding bony looking things that raise her body from the floor.

"What the fuck, what the fuck, what the fuck!?" Travis repeats, more alert with each word.

Lily shudders from the floor with her knees bent and eyes pried open.

Zoe looks at her mommy and as the bony things that hold her up from the carpet begin to move Lily realizes they're what was pinching her.

Legs.

Zoe's body starts to elongate in an impossible movement as those legs press forward against the carpet. Wet spots are left in the carpet from whatever is secreting from Zoe where those legs have grown from her torso. Lily locks eyes with her daughter as she approaches slowly, like Zoe's learning to walk all over again. "Mommy," she says, just as small and innocent as all the times before, but somehow nastier and unfamiliar as well.

Lily pushes her feet into the floor, scaling along the way toward the door as her daughter takes her new first steps toward her.

"Babe! ... Do something!" Travis screams. He climbs down from the dresser.

Zoe's eyes soften at the desire to be held by her mommy. Lily resists the urge to shriek as she watches Zoe's eyes turn from soft blue into a jaundiced cloudy yellow.

"Mommy," Zoe cries, with her stubby arms held out and her fingers clasping open and closed. The desperate reach for a mother's love.

"Do something!" Travis demands as he is on the floor, but sure to keep the bed and a comfortable distance between him and Zoe.

Lily shuffles more and pulls herself up carefully, never taking her eyes off her daughter and what's happening to her. "Baby ... Mommy's just gonna have," Zoe's head tilts to one side. "Mommy just," her voice cracks, finding it difficult to feign the confidence of a protector. "Mommy just needs to have a look, okay baby?" Lily observes Zoe closely with the open hallway at her back where she can run if she needs to. The little legs weave through several new holes in Zoe's *Daddy's Lil' Monster* shirt. "Mommy's so sorry for dropping you, baby," she says through her rattled, but careful voice. Her tone remains inviting and soft.

Travis climbs onto the bed. "Hey ... what are we gonna do? What the hell is even happening?"

"I don't know. Just ... shut up for a second!" Lily snaps.

Zoe creeps toward her more. Lily stands with tears leaking from her eyes as she pretends to be brave and understand her daughter.

Zoe stops.

Her original legs stand as the rest of her horrid body stands upright. The thin and nasty looking legs squirm from her body as Lily gets a good look. Zoe's body begins to elongate and stretch even more. The metamorphosis is unreal. Travis steps off of the bed and is making his way to the door.

Zoe's face goes from stagnant to sad. Her bottom lip puckered out as her eyes tighten and she lets out a roaring cry, not too unlike the cry of her wanting to be fed.

Lily watches, helpless and unsure what to do. Her motherly instinct is to cuddle her and hold her close, but she's scared to death of her own daughter and unsure of what is happening before her eyes. The cry causes Lily and Travis to tense up.

Zoe's little arms reach for her mother. Lily fights the urge to reach back and take her. Zoe's little face melts as Lily's heart breaks. Zoe is now a long and awkward body with more legs growing and tearing from her stretched out torso. The crying quickly is broken by a hiss that tries to cry but sounds like something more primal. Zoe's crying face reddens from the tension of the stretching. Flesh bubbles and boils as it tears and disfigures.

Lily screams at the sight. She falls back into the hallway as she slams against the floor, crawling away as she continues to spectate her daughter's transformation. The hissing sound grows louder as Zoe's mouth widens and rips from the jaw, and the layer of human flesh peels off like sunburn flaking to reveal a grotesque head with black pincers where her mouth once was. The sounds of skin tearing along the hissing is the score to the most morbid of dreams. The yellow in her eyes blackens and the thin tiny legs flutter and reach for Lily. Zoe's chubby baby legs fuse together and snap backwards in a slow and jerking movement. The bones crack and pop as Zoe's legs separate and look like the many legs that have grown, only a bit thicker. Zoe has become something unrecognizable, and something incapable of being loved by some.

Travis scales along the wall afraid, sticking as close to it as he can. Bursting past Zoe as she writhes and hisses, Travis hugs his wife in the hallway. "Are you okay?"

Lily rises back to her feet with the help of Travis. She doesn't speak. She only shakes her head with terror in her eyes.

"We have to do something, Lil," he says with urgency, turning back to his daughter.

"What are we supposed to do!?" Lily asks.

"We have to kill it!"

"It? Are you serious!?" Lily asks in disbelief. "That *it* is our fucking daughter, Travis!"

Travis grabs Lily's hand and looks her in the eye. "Baby ... sweetie ... listen to me ... that's not our daughter anymore."

Zoe crawls into the hallway toward her parents. Her many legs move from the carpeted bedroom floor and over the transition strip in the doorway and onto the wooden floor in the hallway. Each leg clicks against the floor with the slow, creeping slither.

Tick ... tick ... tick ... tick.

Tick, tick ... tick, tick.

Tick.

Travis breaks from Lily and scampers away. Lily backs up with slow steps until she's in the kitchen looking around, unsure if she should try to protect herself or run. *Is Travis right?* she wonders.

Travis rummages around the kitchen counter, tossing hand towels onto the floor, utensils clang and scatter around the drawer before he slams it shut and leaves through the door in the kitchen that goes out to the garage.

Tick, tick, the feet dance in small strides as Zoe moves toward her mother. The pincers on her mouth wagging, opening and closing as she hisses. Liquid seeps from what looks like her mouth, but is just a gaping black hole. Lily flinches at the hissing sound while still trying to look like she's not more frightened than she's ever been in her life. This can't be the same baby girl she watched take her first steps and say her first words.

"Travis!?" she calls out. She holds a hand out defensively as if to ward off Zoe from swallowing her whole with that terrifying mouth with a blackness so deep to stare into that it's impossible to imagine an end ... And those pincers, even more horrific looking. *Maybe Travis was right. Maybe this isn't our little girl anymore,* she thinks as this abomination that Zoe became comes toward her. Her body stretches into something otherworldly, seeming to go on forever as it moves toward her. Lily tries to soften her face with another step backward as she looks into the beady black eyes of her daughter. "Zoe Bear ... baby ... it's Mommy ..."

Tick, tick.

Zoe hisses again.

Tick, tick.

Unable to hold it together, Lily's heart breaks and tears fall. "What happened to you, baby? Why!?"

Travis swings the garage door open and barrels into the kitchen, sweaty and holding a shovel, with determination scrawled on his face. He walks past Lily as if she weren't there at all, with focus fixed on Zoe.

Tick, tick, tick.

"You want me to kill the bug?" Travis asks, to no one in particular, hyping himself to face the bug that his wife was once mortified to even look at. "I'll kill your damn bug!" he growls as he raises the shovel over his head.

"No!" Lily begs, rushing over to grab the shovel before he can bring it down onto their daughter's head.

Travis twists his body, refusing to let go of the shovel. "What are you doing!?" he demands, jerking the shovel away from Lily. Desperate to hold on, Lily is tugged forward, toward Travis as they struggle to have the shovel.

"What am *I* doing?" Lily asks. "What are *you* doing!? That's our daughter!"

Travis stops pulling on the handle and instead shoves Lily back. She falls onto her back and Travis mounts her, pinning her to the floor with the shovel handle against her neck. "That's *not* our daughter anymore. Look at that thing!" he shouts.

Lily surrenders, "Please, stop. Don't hurt me!" she begs with her hands raised.

"I don't want to hurt you. Can't you see? I'm trying to protect you!"

"Please don't hurt Zoe," Lily begs as she begins to hyperventilate. "Don't hurt my baby. Don't hurt our ba–"

Lily feels her husband torn away from her as the shovel drops from Travis' hands and onto Lily. With a yelp, he's taken by Zoe and Lily sits up, pushing herself away with her feet. She gets to her knees and reaches for the shovel and holds it so tight that her knuckles turn white and her palms hurt. She can practically feel the splinters from the handle.

"Lily, help me!" Travis cries. "Help!"

Zoe has her father held within several of her front thin bone legs. She constricts him with a pair of legs that still show signs of Zoe's human hands by the fingers. They still move and coordinate as they grip Travis' shoulders, the same way they would with finger foods.

"No! Stop!"

Lily watches. The horror unfolds as her daughter clicks the pincers together and begins to thrash her husband against the hallway wall and whips her long body up to slam him into the floor like a ragdoll. Each slam rings out with a sickening thud.

"Help!" he pleads.

Boom! Another slam into the wall.

"Please!" he pleads once more as blood is left on the wall, knocking a pair of family photos off their nails as they smash onto the floor, leaving shards of glass around their tattered frames.

Boom! He slams into the opposite wall.

"Lily! Hel–"

Boom! Once more to the other before Travis' body goes limp and his begging ceases.

Lily's bottom lip puckers out and her face tenses up just before breaking. "Noooo!" she screams with a flood of tears. Her shrieking carries into the hallway and she backs away, this time faster. Lily watches from the front door of the house as Zoe pulls her entire body—that nearly spans the sixteen feet length of hallway—out to encircle her father, lying motionless on the floor after being released.

Zoe stands over her father, her head snapping to the floor as the pincers tug and pick at Travis' arm.

"Zoe ... honey," Lily says, her voice softer and more inviting. More ... familiar and loving, even if still noticeably shaken.

Zoe freezes for a moment and her head points toward Lily, as if she understands. Lily's lip quivers as she crouches, unsure how to be motherly anymore with her daughter. This transformation. Everything she's seen. Everything she's feeling. Lily sits on the floor with her knees pulled to her chest, arms hugging her legs as her eyes peek over her knees and stare at what her little baby Zoe has become. The two lock eyes for a moment. Time slows down and Lily sits, lost.

She's jarred as her skeleton jumps within her skin when Zoe's head whips in a flash toward the floor, taking Travis by the head. The pincers are in one ear and the other in his neck as Zoe begins to swallow his head. The pincers retract and help to pull her father's body into that black hole of a mouth. Lily watches, fear-riddled. Zoe's mouth widens more and more under the pincers—and help from the other tiny bony legs—are able to consume the width of his shoulders.

Lily's hands cover her mouth like she's trying to put pressure on a wound, but in this case she only hushes her instinct to scream. Travis's legs bend and kick while muffled screams echo from Zoe's mouth for only a brief few seconds before stopping. His bones crack and he is engulfed within minutes ... all while Mommy watches.

ELEVEN

U nable to unhear the horrid sounds of her husband's demise, she remains on the living room floor in shock. Her hands fall to her side as her vision is obstructed by the tears. Her heart still rages. The hallway is in her view as she spaces out in that general direction. The blurry shape of Zoe snakes low.

Tick tick tick as her legs click across the floor, coming closer to her mother. The clicking and skittering steps stop as Zoe's lengthy body drops lower to be beside her mother. Lily's thousand-yard stare remains unbroken. Something in her compels her to not be frightened. Zoe's head nuzzles up to her, brushing against her slack arm, similar to how a dog or a cat might do when they want attention. How a child would their mother when they need comfort and love.

Zoe gently places one of her thin and pointy legs on Lily's thigh with a non-threatening pressure before collapsing comfortably beside her mother. Her body rests on the living room floor like an imaginary large snake with legs.

As Lily slowly moves her head and lets her eyes crawl along and study her baby's changed body, she notices the obviously engorged part of Zoe's body. Lily inhales big through her nose and lets it out from her mouth realizing exactly what that is. She raises her hand and hesitantly places it on Zoe, running her fingertips along the base of one of her pincers. The two sit like this until Lily nods off.

Lily awakens in the same position as before, her head slumped over and resting on Zoe's body. The afternoon sunlight illuminates the house, pouring in from the kitchen and living room windows. "Let Mommy up, baby," she whispers as she moves Zoe's head off of her and readjusts her legs away so she can stand. Zoe's body squirms but she stays on the floor.

As Lily gets to her feet an excruciating pain takes hold of her, insisting she hunch over and clutch her stomach. "Aaaagggghhhh!"

She only manages a few steps before plummeting to her knees and meagerly holding herself up with her forehead against the floor. Her breathing is in short bursts with vocal exhales and sporadic cries of pain. The pain travels through her body in an unfamiliar way, but she manages to catch her wind and get back to her feet and lurch her way into the bathroom. She feels nauseous and leans over where the toilet welcomes her, waiting to accept the gifts that her body rejects, but nothing happens. Her stomach tightens and flexes and her throat convulses to no desired end result.

She stands in front of the sink and has a look at herself in the mirror. The pain radiating from her face suggests that she take a look at her skin where the pain is. Slowly, she pulls up the shirt, the fabric brushing against her sensitive skin—that feels sunburnt—only causes her to wince and be more careful. At the first glimpse of exposed flesh she can see the redness. Angry flesh in need of soothing. As she gets the shirt up above her bra, she notices her stomach and rib cage. Something is moving, pressing against her skin like it's trying to get out. Her eyes widen and before she can scream the skin tears in multiple places on her body. Thin, bony legs extend from her body—just like Zoe's—and as she stares into her face in the mirror her cloudy jaundiced eyes stare back just before a terrifying scream is released, breaking the peaceful silence of their loving home.

ACKNOWLEDGEMENTS

This short story was the result of my horrific imagination feeling playful. This was an idea that I wanted to explore that takes the common dynamic between couples where typically the wife or girlfriend are scared of bugs to a point that the husband or boyfriend is expected to kill the bugs for her. I have been in this relationship, and many many others have too. I wanted to play with this real life dynamic and this story, **Kill ~~the bugs~~ For Me**, is what came of it. I want to give a massive, thirty-legged shout out to those of you on the side of the relationship afraid of bugs. (Even if you're a guy squealing over bugs, I see you and you can still be a king.)

A special loving thanks to my lady who may or may not also be petrified of bugs ... this is about me thanking Kaylynn, not poking fun at her for not liking spiders and anything that moves. I love you and I'm sorry that I find spiders and other bugs so fascinating.

A special hissing shout out to my beta readers.

Danielle Morris. Your stream of reactions and positive notes among the constructive bits were a highlight of the revising process. I think every writer needs a beta reader like you in their corner.

Mo Medusa. I appreciate you so much. Your expertise in craft is invaluable and I have so much respect for you and am thankful that you took time to read about Lily and Travis.

Kirsten Noelle Craig. I appreciate you cheerleading my writing and providing great notes along the way. Your reactions in the live document made me laugh.

Karly Latham. Thank you for being an unexpected reader for this. I was thrilled to share this with you and get your insight and you didn't disappoint. Your comments and reactions were fun to read through and validating of the positive marks in the first draft. Thank you!

Michael Nunn. A talented writer and one of the friendliest people I know in this space. For someone who has never beta read before this story, you nailed it. I will forever be insecure about my characters showering and stinky moving forward.

Jason A. Jones. Your insight as a horror reader and proficient writer is of high value. I always feel a confidence boost when you give a nod of approval to anything silly I write. Big thanks!

A slithering thanks to Joey Powell for the sick illustration and entire book design. I mean seriously, whoever is reading this, did you see the cover? If you somehow missed it, stop reading this and look real quick. ... see what I mean? Anyhoo, thanks Joey! Not only for the visuals and presentation of this story, but for just being an overall kind and supportive friend in this space. More people need a Joey Powell in their corner.

And lastly, **thank you** to all the readers who read and talk about my writing. I always love to talk about my brand of horror and love when I am tagged in things on social media. It truly fills my cup and I'm convinced that the feeling that you provide me will never get old. I hope you enjoyed this one as much as I did writing it.

ABOUT THE AUTHOR

David lives in the Greater Cincinnati area (in Northern Kentucky for any locals who choose to argue about geography) where he lives with his two teen sons and the lady of the house. When David isn't fighting imposter syndrome as a writer he is probably working out, watching horror movies, baseball, or wrestling.

Suspense and Tension are David's playground and he has independently self-published multiple books in addition to having short stories published in several anthologies.

OTHER PUBLISHED WORK

Novels

Devils That Prey

DIY Exorcism

Novellas

The Tickle Monster

Features

HorrorScope: A Zodiac Anthology, Vol.2.

Curbside Curses: The Yardsale Anthology

Till the Yule Log Burns Out

(THE POST CREDIT SCENE)

P aul pulls up to the final house on his route. His sprinter van, once full of packages, emptied out and delivered across multiple cities in just under six hours. Not as much of a testament to his work ethic as much as how much he just wants to go home. The afternoon sun rages against the hot van making him thankful for that cool AC in the main cabin. He puts the van in *park* and slides himself through to the back where he grabs the last package of the day and scans it with his mobile handheld scanner.

"Ugh," he says with an eye roll.

Signature required, it displays after he hits the barcode.

Paul slides open the side panel door and steps out where the high sun kisses his skin with an immediate wall of heat. He leaves the van running so that the cool air is there to greet him when he returns. Cutting through the grass, he ignores the paved walk path that leads to the front door, charting a path of his own. He steps onto the front stoop, able to skip the three stairs with one long stride up. With the scanner on the signature screen still he knocks on the door. Five taps of his knuckles play against the door with a melody universally known.

Knock, kn-kn-knock-knock

The door seems to already be open as the knob clicks and the door slowly creeps open to reveal a dark living room. "Hey, uh ... I got a delivery," he begins. "I'm sorry, the door just opened when I knocked."

The door continues to slowly open before stopping. Paul pops his head inside to let his eyes focus on the darkness. "Hello?" he beckons into the living room as his voice rings back at him. The package rests under his arm while the scanner is clutched in his opposite hand.

For only a moment, Paul looks around outside. Maybe for a neighbor, or whoever lives at the house. He sees the car in the driveway and turns to face the street. It would be so easy for him to just drop the package on the doorstep and keep it moving, but the damn signature required complicates things. Of course it's the last package of the day too.

The quiet is only broken by the running motor of the van.

Paul releases a loud exhale, "Where the hell is any-one?" he whispers under his breath, studying the houses across the street. His peaceful observations are disrupted... *tick, tick,* he hears, coming from inside the house. He turns around to gaze inside. Again, he tries to focus.

Tick tick tick tick tick tick tick tick.

Must be a dog, he thinks.

He pops his head back in with a single foot stepping onto the threshold. "I have your package, I just need a signature."

Ticktick

tickticktick tick tick tick tick

tickticktickticktickticktickticktricktcktcktckckckckckckckck-ck.

The sounds move at an impossibly fast speed he realizes. He nudges the door open wider and before he can see what's making the sound grow louder and closer he feels himself pulled violently into the house with a stifled cry as the front door slams shut to the world outside. The package and scanner hit the floor and are pushed outside to be left on the porch as screams fill the other side of the door before abrupt silence is all that remains.

Stay connected with David Washburn.
Say "hello."
www.WashburnWrites.com
Instagram | Threads
@WashburnWrites

If you enjoyed this story, please rate and review any-
where you can rate and review books.
Amazon and GoodReads are a great place to start.
This really helps out independent authors more than
you know.
Thanks for reading.

www.ingramcontent.com/pod-product-compliance
Lightning Source LLC
Chambersburg PA
CBHW020121310726
48970CB00002B/742